ice sports

OLYMPIC SPORTS

robert sandelson

Crestwood House
New York

Maxwell Macmillan International
New York   Oxford   Singapore   Sydney

OLYMPIC SPORTS

TRACK ATHLETICS
FIELD ATHLETICS
SWIMMING AND DIVING
GYMNASTICS
ICE SPORTS
SKIING
BALL SPORTS
COMBAT SPORTS

Designer: Ross George
Editor: Deborah Elliott

Cover: An outstanding moment in Olympic history. In Lake Placid in 1980, the United States played the Soviet Union in one of the greatest-ever ice hockey semifinals. Here, the two teams shake hands sportingly before the game.

Crestwood House
Macmillan Publishing Company
866 Third Avenue
New York, NY 10022

Macmillan Publishing Company is part of the Maxwell Communication Group of Companies.

First published in Great Britain in 1991
by Wayland (Publishers) Ltd
61 Western Road, Hove, East Sussex BN3 1JD

Printed in Italy by G. Canale & C.S.p.A.
1 2 3 4 5 6 7 8 9 10

ACKNOWLEDGMENTS

The Publisher would like to thank the following agencies and photographers for allowing their photographs to be reproduced in this book: All Sport UK Ltd 12, 27, 43 (Don Morley); BBC Hulton Picture Library 6, 13–16, 40; Colorsport *cover*, 10–11 17–19, 24, 26, 28–30 (both), 32–33 (top), 34–36, 38, 44–45; Topham Picture Library 5, 7–9, 21–23, 25, 31, 33 (bottom), 39, 41–42.

Library of Congress Cataloging-in-Publication Data

Sandelson, Robert.
   Ice Sports/Robert Sandelson — 1st ed...
       p.   cm. — (Olympic sports)
   Includes index.
   Summary: Presents a history of ice sports competition in the Olympic Games, featuring bobsledding, ice hockey, figure skating, pairs skating, ice dancing and speed skating.
ISBN 0-89686-667-X
   1. Winter sports — Juvenile literature.
   2. Winter Olympics — History — Juvenile literature. [1. Winter Sports. 2. Winter Olympics. — History.] I. Title. II. Series
GV841.S26   1991
796.9—dc20   91-3881

CONTENTS

THE WINTER GAMES

The history of ice sports at the Olympics starts, ironically, in the summer. The 1908 Games held in London had skating events, though they were absent from the program four years later in Stockholm, Sweden. This seemed strange because Sweden boasted many of the world's top skating stars. Skating was revived in Antwerp, Belgium, in 1920. A total of seventy-three men and twelve women from ten different countries gathered in the Ice Palace. Four years later the Winter Games had their own home in Chamonix, France. The ice competitions have been a cornerstone of Olympic entertainment ever since.

The variety of ice sports is enormous. It ranges from the elegance of figure skating, to the power and grace of speedskating, to the rough-tough danger of ice hockey. The Winter Olympic competitions have rewarded us with brilliant performances on ice — balletic and strong, fast and nimble.

For audiences, however, ice sports do not seem to carry as much appeal or hold as much glamor as the events in the Summer Games. Speedskating, for example, is a little known and rarely talked of sport. Yet the world's greatest speedskater, Eric Heiden, has won more individual gold medals in one Games than the famous swimmer Mark Spitz. In the 1980s, thanks greatly to Britain's Jayne Torvill and Christopher Dean, ice skating experienced a revival. The couple's perfection in the ice dancing competition, culminating in a gold-medal-winning performance in 1984, brought fans into the skating arena.

Ice hockey is probably the most popular ice sport. However, this may be because of its violent nature.

▲ Jayne Torvill and Christopher Dean from England have successfully promoted the Winter Olympics with their breathtaking ice dancing displays. Here they are pictured during their famous *Bolero* routine at the 1984 Games in Sarajevo, Yugoslavia.

▶ A Winter Olympics mural in Calgary, Canada, in 1988.

BOBSLEDDING

Bobsledding is a fast and sometimes dangerous sport. Each team of two or four people climbs into a sled, which looks something like a bathtub on skates, and storms down an ice channel at speeds of up to 100 mph (160 kph). The driver sits at the front and has some control over the direction of the sled. He or she is the most vulnerable in the event of an accident.

The two-man bobsled competition was first held in 1932 in Lake Placid. The winners were brothers Curtis and J. Hubert Stevens. They had discovered that hot runners travel more quickly over the ice than ordinary runners. (Runners are the thin blades at the bottom of the sled.) Armed with this knowledge, the brothers heated their runners with blowtorches. Of course the theory proved successful because a skate's movement on ice depends on its friction melting the surface. The artificial melting of ice with hot skates reduces the need for friction, which normally creates heat but also slows the skate. This practice is

▼ The first round of the bobsled competition at Chamonix in 1924 was marked by a bad accident. The Swiss team (pictured below) capsized and went off the track.

▲ Lamberto Dalla Costa (front) and Giacomo Conti of Italy won the two-man bobsled event in front of a home crowd at the 1956 Games in Cortina d'Ampezzo, Italy.

now highly illegal, since it would make the skill of heating the runners more important than the racing itself. The temptation remains, though, and for some competitors it has sometimes been too great to resist.

Another way of increasing the speed of bobsleds is to use heavy team members. The average weight of the German bobsledders in 1952 in Oslo, Norway, was 260 lb (118 kg). A weight limit was then introduced, which meant the average weight per racer could be no more than 220 lb (100 kg) — still no featherweights!

The competitive spirit of the top athletes means that great risks are largely ignored. Also, unlike many other sports, age is not a barrier, so competitors can race for years. Of all sports, bobsledding boasts some of the oldest competitors. For example, Italian Giacomo Conti won an Olympic title at the age of forty-seven!

The tenacity of these athletes is displayed in the story of Eugenio Monti, also of Italy. He was World Champion ten times. But the title of Olympic Champion eluded him for many years. His best attempts never seemed to be quite good enough for the gold medal.

As a member of one of the best two teams in Cortina d'Ampezzo in 1956, he was narrowly beaten into second place.

Eight years later in Innsbruck, Austria, he seemed assured of victory. His great rivals, Tony Nash and Robin Dixon of the British team, had a broken sled. Monti, however, preferred not to win by default. He helped the British team to complete their round by sending them the spare part they needed. Nash and Dixon duly completed their runs and won the gold medal.

At the next Games, in Grenoble, France, in 1968, the success that is said to come to all those who wait came to Monti. At the age of forty, he and his partner broke the course record. Although their combined time was equaled by another team, they were given the gold because they had produced the single fastest run.

▼ Italian bobsledder Eugenio Monti gets a sympathetic pat from Mrs. Robin Dixon. Monti was beaten in the two-man bobsled competition by Mrs. Dixon's husband and his partner, Tony Nash, in 1964 in Innsbruck.

Monti was happy to retire as ten-time World Champion and now Olympic Champion. Presumably, he was also relieved that he had accomplished safely all he had wanted in the most dangerous sport in the Olympics. The dangers are obvious. But competitors must push such thoughts to the back of their minds. Felix Endrich, the 1948 Olympic Champion in St. Moritz, France, had no intention of retiring when he won the gold medal at the age of twenty-six.

▲ Britain's Tony Nash (left) and Robin Dixon celebrate their victory.

But five years later, on the world championship course at Garmisch-Partenkirchen, Germany, he died when, as the driver, his sled went over the wall at a difficult curve and hit a tree.

One of the most brilliant of cross-over sportspeople (athletes who excel in more than one sport) was Edward Eagan. Eagan was the only man to win gold medals in both Winter and

Summer Olympic Games. In the 1920 Summer Games in Antwerp, he won the light heavyweight boxing gold medal. Twelve years later in Lake Placid he was a member of the illustrious four-man bobsled team that won the gold medal.

The sled was driven by Billy Fiske. Fours years earlier in St. Moritz, at the age of only sixteen, Fiske had driven a team to victory. This made him one of the youngest gold medal winners in the history of the Winter Olympics. On the same team was forty-eight-year-old Jay O'Brien. He held the record as the oldest Winter Games gold medalist. Bad weather delayed the start of the competition until after the official end of the Games. The American team, led by Fiske, raced well that day.

Edwin Moses, two-time Olympic gold medalist in the 400-m hurdles and probably the greatest hurdler the world has ever seen, entered the bobsled competition in the Olympics in 1992 to try to equal Eagan's achievement.

▼ Irina Koussakina of the Soviet Union at the start of the women's luge in Calgary in 1988.

Luge is also known as the toboggan. The luge is an even more dangerous version of the bobsled. The racer goes down feet first, pulling a strap attached to the front runner to steer. It was first included in the Olympic program in Innsbruck in 1964. Spectators were shocked to see the tobogganists adopt a sitting position and then lean back to decrease resistance. This was in total contrast to the forward-leaning style of the bobsled and the Cresta run. However, it soon became apparent that the luge was an immensely exciting sport to watch.

In 1968 in Grenoble the first and

▲ American Cameron Myler demonstrates the speed and danger of the luge as she flies past the audience in the women's competition in Calgary. Myler finished the competition in ninth place overall.

second places in the women's individual luge went to two East Germans. But it was a sad reflection on their overzealous competitiveness when the two were disqualified for heating the runners on their sleds. The gold medal went instead to the Italian third-place finisher Erica Lechner.

ICE HOCKEY

The origins of ice hockey are clouded in controversy. One claim is that it began in Canada during the 1800s. Another is that it is an offshoot of an ancient English game called "Bandy." Wherever it started or whatever it once was, ice hockey is one of the world's fastest team games. The puck flies across the ice in excess of 100 mph (160 kph), and players need quick reflexes and protective padding. The teams are made up of six players, with reserves for substitutions.

The first Olympic competition took place in Antwerp in 1920. This was not only an Olympic celebration but also the first-ever World Championship. Subsequently, from 1924 to 1972, the Olympic Games were also seen as World Championships (except in 1932). The reason for this was the enormous expense of teams traveling long distances. After 1972, when financial sponsorship became more widely available, the arrangement ended, and the tournaments became separate. Finally, in 1976 different

▼ An early example of an ice hockey game. It is taking place on a frozen lake rather than the more secure modern indoor rink.

Canada beat the United States by 6–1 in the final in Chamonix in 1924.

tournaments were held for professional and amateur teams.

Over the years the dominant teams have been from the Soviet Union and Canada. From the very beginning the Canadians were *the* team to beat. However, following its entry in 1956 in Cortina d'Ampezzo, Italy, the Soviet Union became the dominant force. Considering its climate, it is easy to see why Canada had such good ice hockey teams. Their leagues and players not only led the world, sometimes their players even played for the other competing countries. In 1920, while the Canadians held a competition to find the top team to represent them at the Olympics — the Winnipeg Falcons — Britain was unable even to raise one team. In 1924 in Chamonix, the British team had nine Canadians and just two Britons. Even so, having the Canadians play for you is not the same as being the Canadian team. In that year the Canadians won the gold, beating Switzerland 33–0, Britain 19–2, and the United States in the final, 6–1.

▲ The victorious Canadian ice hockey team in 1924 — the Winnipeg Falcons.

Canada won again in 1928 in St. Moritz and in 1932 in Lake Placid. The competition, however, was strengthening by this time. In a play-off against Canada, the American team members found themselves a goal ahead only minutes away from a stunning upset. But the Canadians clawed their way back for the tie they needed to ensure their victory. This proved to be an ominous sign. Four years later, Canada's twenty-year stranglehold was dramatically broken by a country that could not even afford to send an ice hockey team in 1932 — Britain.

The popularity of ice hockey was growing in Britain. More rinks opened and were available to hockey players as well as figure skaters and speed skaters. When an ice rink opened in London, it enjoyed royal patronage from the Duke of York, a keen sports fan, who became King George VI. He came to play the new exciting sport. Ice hockey leagues began to flourish throughout Britain. It was in this atmosphere that the British team assembled for the 1936 Games in Garmisch-Partenkirchen, Germany.

Before the ice hockey competition began, the International Ice Hockey Federation banned Jimmy Foster and Alec Archer from playing on the British team. Both had played hockey in Canada. However, since the two players were British citizens, objections to their playing could not be justified. The suspension was lifted amid accusations of bias from the American team and Olympic officials.

As it turned out, Foster played a vital role in the Olympic competition. He

▼ The American and Canadian teams were top contenders for the ice hockey gold medal at the Games in 1936 in Garmisch-Partenkirchen. Britain was the surprise winner, however. Here, Canada and the United States battle for the silver and bronze medals.

was a brilliant goalkeeper perhaps the best in the history of the game. His ability to keep a shutout (prevent a score) led to his being known affectionately by fellow players and spectators as the "Shutout King."

The British captain, Carl Erhardt, a veteran at thirty-nine, had brought his team up to world standards. It cruised through the opening rounds to reach the semifinal match against the mighty Canadian team unbeaten. The British scored a goal from a long shot after only 40 seconds of play. Under pressure, the Canadians tied the game — the first goal that Foster had given up in the tournament. Suddenly the Canadians looked invincible to almost everyone but their opponents.

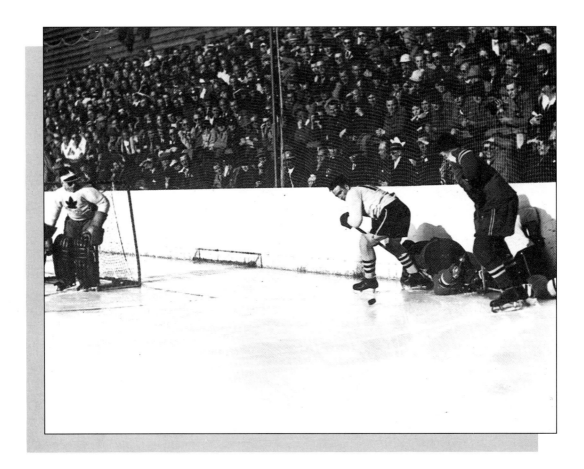

The British team began to struggle. However, their brilliant defense, and Foster's determination not to let another puck past him, meant the game was far from over. As the last period started, the Canadians threw every player forward in a desperate attempt to score. This proved to be their undoing. Their remorseless attacking left their own defenses weak. When two British forwards broke for goal the Canadians could only look in despair as a shot was deflected by their goalkeeper only to be put away by another forward. The score at the end was 2−1 for the British. The

▲ Britain's shock victory against Canada in 1936 resulted in the team going on to win gold. The Canadians could manage only second place with the United States in third.

Canadian domination might have been over, but the Olympic gold medal was still to be decided.

The British and Canadian teams went on to beat the Czechs 5−0 and 7−0 respectively. (The British win secured them the European title.) All then depended on the match between the United States and Britain. It was a historic occasion for the British. The game ended in a scoreless tie, 0−0.

The British had virtually secured the other two titles that make up the "Triple Crown," the world and Olympic titles.

The Canadians beat the American team to secure a second place silver medal. British ice hockey players were on top of the world. Goalkeeper Jimmy Foster was widely credited as making the difference between the British team and all the others. His four Olympic shutouts in seven games was a brilliant achievement.

For a brief period before and after World War II, the Canadians regained their supremacy. However, the Soviets appeared as a force on the scene, and Canada's days of Olympic domination were over. The Soviet teams made a strong impression on the world of ice hockey, especially for their sportsmanship and style. In their first attempt, in Cortina d'Ampezzo in 1956, the Soviet team won the Olympic gold medal. Four years later, in Squaw Valley, California, in front of a wildly partisan crowd and against a wildly inspired American team, they were defeated.

This was the Soviet Union's first defeat by the United States but by no means the most famous. In the years to come the Soviet stranglehold was as tight as Canada's had once been.

▼ The American goalkeeper lunges to try to stop a shot on goal from a Soviet striker.

The most famous victory in Olympic ice hockey, after the totally unexpected British victory in 1936, was the American victory over the Soviets in Lake Placid in 1980. Before the Games started the Soviet team had beaten the U.S. Olympic team 10 – 3, as well as the NHL All-Stars. The United States was seeded seventh out of twelve and was lucky to make even seventh. But during the first game against Sweden the players began to rise to the occasion. At 2 – 1 down and looking to be worthy of the low estimate put on their skill, they managed to come back and escape with a tie. Their confidence began to increase against the Czech team, and they caused an upset by winning 7 – 3. Now, their momentum was gathering. The team continued to make comebacks. In seven games the Americans scored first only once! Victories followed, and a confident team took the ice against the mighty Soviets. The match appeared to be going as expected with the Soviets leading from the start. The Americans, though, were never more than one goal behind and began the last period at 3 – 2 down. Two quick goals from the American team and the unbelievable happened. Although stunned, the losing Soviet team congratulated the American victors.

▶ Side-by-side in battle: The United States versus the Soviet Union in 1980.

▼ This photograph shows some of the images considered typical of modern ice hockey — mass celebrations together with a heated, physical brawl.

FIGURE SKATING

The single figure skater is arguably the most dynamic sight in the Winter Olympics. As he or she spins, swoops, drops, and rises over the ice the audience is enraptured by the control and deliberation in every move. So well do the competitors know their routines that they make it look almost effortless. Yet we know that such brilliance is hard-won: Bruised legs and arms as well as physical and mental exhaustion are the prices that solo skaters must pay for brilliance. If they fall while practicing a new move they must pick themselves up, ignore the pain, and try again to create that exquisite move.

In the late 1800s, skating was popular among both men and women. The emphasis in those days was on the perfect execution of the compulsory figures on the ice. Technical expertise was tested before anything else. In the first International Championships in Hamburg in 1891 there was no freestyle skating program at all. This represented the strong belief in the supremacy of figures above all else in the sport. For some, this attitude persisted for a long time. Many years later, in 1982, when Karl Schäfer did a blur-spin (a spin that is fast enough to blur the eye), he was criticized for being circuslike! Under these strictures men and women were able to compete, as in other events, on an equal footing.

The greatest of the early skaters were Florence Madeline-Syers of Britain, who was known affectionately as "Madge," and Ulrich Salchow of Sweden. In 1902 Madge entered the World Championships in London and competed against men. She came extremely close to winning. Only Salchow was able to beat her in the end.

Salchow gave his name to the now famous jump. In a "Salchow," a skater takes off from the back inside edge of one skate, makes a complete turn in the air, and lands on the back outside edge of the opposite skate.

Madge caused such an upset that separate events were organized to prevent women from beating men. The first separate events were held in 1906. Two years later the first Olympic competition took place during the 1908 London Games. There were twenty skaters from six countries: the Soviet Union, Germany, the United States, Argentina, Britain, and Sweden.

Madge came out of retirement at the age of twenty-seven to win the gold medal in the singles. She also won the bronze in the pairs competition, skating with her husband, Edgar. This proved her versatility and talent beyond all doubt. It also showed, once again,

▶ The brilliant Sonja Henie of Norway won the women's individual skating titles in 1928, 1932, and 1936.

that women skaters could be as technically accomplished and physically capable as men. In the separate men's competition, Salchow beat Nicolai Panin of the Soviet Union in controversial circumstances. Panin accused the judges of being biased, a charge that has since been often heard in this sport. The problem arises from the fact that whenever judges are required to give their opinion, accusations of bias are inevitable. The upset Panin, who a few months earlier had been the first man to beat Salchow in six years, stormed out of the competition.

This Olympic competition was held as part of the 1908 Summer Games in London and in 1920 in Antwerp but not, surprisingly, in Stockholm in 1912, and not in 1916 because of World War I. The separate Winter competition did not start in earnest until 1924 in Chamonix.

Salchow's successor to the title in Antwerp was another Swede, Gillis Grafström. Salchow, at the age of forty-two, finished in fourth place. Grafström went on to dominate skating by winning the title at the 1924 and 1928 Games. He was also the originator of the flying sit spin. This jump starts from a forward outside edge of a skate. The skater squats on one foot and extends the other in front. In 1932 Grafström finished second after crashing into a movie camera that was set too near the rink. This accident, combined with a terrible

▲ Sonja Henie arrives in New York in 1936 having retired from skating and seeking a Hollywood film contract.

lapse of concentration in the compulsory figures, almost certainly prevented him from taking a fourth title.

Sonja Henie

In 1924 in Chamonix one of the most famous skaters of all time took part in her first Olympics — finishing last! Sonja Henie was born in Norway in 1912. Her precocious ability on skates was encouraged by her parents. At the age of twelve she was the Norwegian champion and so entered Olympic competition. On a snowy day in Chamonix, when other contestants were unwilling to take to the ice, she pushed through the crowds onto the rink. It was Henie's first demonstration of her winning personality. Also, because of her age, she was able to wear short skirts and escape the censure that forced older women to wear ankle-length skirts.

Her lack of experience meant that she finished last, but her future looked bright. The winner in Chamonix, however, was the excellent Austrian skater Herma Planck-Szabo. Henie was the runner-up to Planck-Szabo in the 1926 World Championships. In the following year Henie broke the Austrian's ten-year unbeaten record and established her own.

The World Championships were held at Henie's home rink in Oslo. Accusations of partisan voting were raised because three of the five judges were Norwegian. They all voted for Henie. In the protest that followed, a rule was made that disallowed more than one judge per country in a competition. This rule still stands. In 1932 Henie won the gold medal at the Olympics in Lake Placid by an over-whelming margin.

At the 1936 Games in Garmisch-Partenkirchen, her supremacy was under assault from a very talented English girl, Cecilia Colledge. Colledge also knew how to please a crowd, and her Nazi salute was perfect for those who sought favor at the Olympic celebrations of that year — Hitler was in the crowd. But Henie, due to turn

▲ The young British skater Cecilia Colledge challenged Sonja Henie for the Olympic title in 1936.

professional after the Olympics, wanted to end her amateur career on a high note. She, presumably, was planning a career in the movies. All went well as she beat the less-experienced Colledge and then went on to star in her first movie — *One in a Million*. It is said that she was assisted in winning the gold medal by the flattering spotlights that were turned on for her performance as dusk fell.

Katarina Witt of Germany is the greatest modern woman skater.

emerge since Sonja Henie is probably Katarina Witt from Germany. Named second in the list of world sportswomen of the 1980s, her success has been amazing. She is known for her athleticism and her triple jumps. Her victories in the 1980s speak for themselves. She won the Olympic title in 1984 in Sarajevo and again in 1988 in Calgary, and she won the World Championships four times between 1984 and 1988.

World War II affected the Canadians and Americans far less than the Europeans. Competitors from the two countries made their mark as soon as competitions began again. On the men's singles scene, one American skater distinguished himself by pioneering more and more difficult jumps that tested both the strength and nerve of the skater. Dick Button was an eighteen-year-old college student when he first completed the double Axel. This is a very difficult jump requiring two and a half mid-air rotations. Although he had not quite mastered it, Button was never able to duck a challenge. And, as it so often happens, fortune favored the brave. He was awarded first place by eight out of the nine judges. In the years to come Button became the first man ever to perform a triple loop in the Olympic competition, winning the gold in 1952 in Oslo, Norway.

The effect of these lights was dramatic. Lighting is thought to be so influential that, nowadays, a rule specifies that the lighting must stay the same for all contestants.

Henie was a phenomenon. She made skating wildly popular. Young girls, attracted by her short skirts and white leather boots, created a craze by dressing like their idol. Such was her fame that huge crowds turned up to watch and take part in figure skating. As the first skater to become an international celebrity, Henie's influence on the sport cannot be underestimated.

The greatest woman skater to

▲ After his victory in Oslo in 1952, Dick Button turned professional.

It must be remembered that until recently the most famous part of figure skating was not actually figure skating! The figures are intricate movements on ice that were a large part of the competition but were of virtually no interest to audiences. They were usually performed in an empty rink before the freestyle program began. The system used to divide the scoring was 50 percent for figures and 50 percent for the freestyle program. After 1972 the proportions were changed to make the freestyle portion more important.

At the 1972 Olympics in Sapporo, Japan, Trixie Schuba made a virtually perfect set of figures. That meant that going into the second round she was unbeatable. Although she came only seventh in the freestyle program she still won the gold medal. This seemed unacceptable because, after all, it is the freestyle program that people watch. They feel cheated if, in effect, it counts for so little. As a result, the proportions were altered to 40 percent for figures and 60 percent for the freestyle program. In 1988, the compulsories were eliminated completely.

In the years following his reign, Dick Button's athleticism was widely imitated. It became the mainstay of the men's freestyle program. To many people it became a substitute for refined skill or elegance. Dick Button's influence on the freestyle program was first significantly challenged by Britain's John Curry.

John Curry

Through sheer ability John Curry shook the skating world and forced judges to accept his more balletic style.

John Curry practices for the 1976 Olympics in Innsbruck, Austria.

He compromised only when some judges seemed determined to mark him down for not doing certain jumps. These jumps satisfied their demands for a more athletic and technical routine. Curry was never happy to adopt this style, but he would always look out for his own best interests. Therefore, he did the jumps that the judges wanted.

Curry was always a good athlete at

school, spending a lot of his time dancing. At the age of seven he was taken to the Summerhill ice rink where he immediately showed a flair for skating. His first ice skating session lasted only fifteen minutes but Curry was hooked.

The following Christmas, while the family was vacationing in Aldeburgh, on England's east coast, a local lake froze over. Remembering how much he loved the ice, Curry's parents bought him some skates. He happily skated off, but a near accident on the thin ice convinced his parents to take him to the local rink in the future. Since this was safe, his mother and father felt much happier.

Curry's early competitive years were tough. He lacked the sponsorship the American skaters had, and, therefore, he had to depend on many people for their continued support. The most remarkable of his benefactors was Ed Mosler. Mosler was well known for supporting young American skaters. He was so impressed by Curry's performance in the 1972 World Championships that he decided to sponsor him.

Eventually all Curry's hard work paid off. The 1976 season belonged to him as he won the European, Olympic, and World Championships. Winning this grand slam was a great achievement, overcoming as he did the prejudices of the Eastern bloc judges, who favored the more traditional skating style.

Curry later described his experience on going into the Olympic arena as the British team's flag-bearer: ''Of all the competitions I had ever been in, from the hop, skip, and jump event when I was seven, I had never been more in awe of winning anything than I was of winning that gold medal.''

Curry turned professional at the end of that season. He was then able to concentrate more fully on the artistic side of his work — all because of the financial security he had won with the Olympic title. However, following quickly in his footsteps was another British skater, Robin Cousins.

▼ John Curry revolutionized men's figure skating with his ballet style and artistically choreographed routines.

Robin Cousins

Robin Cousins owes his career perhaps as much to embarrassment as to luck! One day while on vacation, the young Cousins was out with his mother and father. Since it was hot, his mother decided to visit an ice rink. She asked a nearby stranger for help to get Cousins on the ice. The stranger turned out to be a coach who demanded money for a lesson for Cousins. His mother was too embarrassed to say no. So she paid what was, at that time, a considerable sum. The little boy took so easily to the ice that the instructor could not believe he had not skated before. He made it clear to Cousins' mother that here was a child with natural talent.

Like John Curry, Cousins had already excelled at dancing. His next natural step would have been to go to the Royal School of Ballet, where he had been offered a scholarship. Thanks to his mother's embarrassment, things went differently. Luckily, a rink soon opened in their home town of Bristol. Now Cousins was able to follow his new passion.

Cousins' route to the top was by no means easy. In 1976 he had painful operations on his knee for cartilage problems. He went to train in Denver, Colorado, near Scott Hamilton, who was to succeed him as the Olympic Champion in 1984. It had long been thought that his erratic scores in the compulsory figures would have a detrimental effect on Cousins' chances of major honors. As with Curry, however, his day would come. In 1980 he won the European Championships. Soon after, in front of 4.5 million British viewers who had stayed up all night to watch the final televised live from Lake Placid, Cousins turned the story of his mom's embarrassment into a fairy tale.

◀ ▲ Robin Cousins took over from fellow Britain John Curry as the Olympic men's figure skating champion. Also, like Curry, Cousins concentrated on the artistic aspect of figure skating — no one could argue with his technical mastery of sport. His skating routines brought fans crowding into arenas to watch him perform.

▲ Scott Hamilton of the United States performs his gold-medal-winning routine in the men's figure skating freestyle program in 1984 in Sarajevo, Yugoslavia.

▼ The winner's podium for the men's figure skating event at the Games in Calgary in 1988. From left to right: Brian Orser (silver), Brian Boitano (gold), and Victor Petrenko (bronze).

PAIRS SKATING

P airs skating involves the harmonious interaction of two skaters. The sport is athletic and spectacular but, ironically, has been put under pressure by its greatest stars — Lyudmila Belousova, Oleg Protopopov and Irina Rodnina. The three brilliant Soviet skaters were vital members of the winning teams in the Games in 1964, 1968, 1972, 1976, and 1980.

Pairs skating is thought to have originated in the 1890s. The first contest did not take place until the Olympic year of 1908, making it one of the rare sports whose history is only as old as the modern Olympic Games. The famous Madge Syers and her husband, Edgar, won the bronze medal in a competition that was won by a German couple, Anna Hubler and Heinrich Burger. The Soviet domination of the event began in 1964 in Innsbruck, Austria. Lyudmila Belousova and her husband, Oleg Protopopov, won the gold medal. They won it again at the 1968 Games in Grenoble.

The two skaters had met on a rink, fell in love, and got married. Then they began to skate together. Their passion for both skating and each other made them inseparable — a quality they always emphasized. Protopopov once said in a fit of exasperation at having continually to compete against brother and sister teams: ''These pairs of brothers and sisters, how can they convey the emotion, the love, that exists between a man and a woman?''

The couple lifted pairs skating to a new high by refusing to repeat figures

▲ Husband and wife team Lyudmila Belousova and Oleg Protopopov won gold medals in 1964 and 1968.

and never resorting to the dull ''shadow skating.'' Their use of choreography lifted the quality of their program to an art form. Their only competition also came from the Soviet Union in the form of the diminutive but brilliant Irina Rodnina. Rodnina and her partner Aleksei Ulanov were instrumental in developing acrobatic leaps and other stunts. By this explosive display of skill and agility they unseated the reigning Protopopovs in the 1969 European Championships.

The particular circumstance that led to this unseating arose because after 1968 the scoring balance between the figure and the free skating programs was altered to have equal importance. The Protopopovs, unbeatable in the figures, found themselves challenged by the younger and more dynamic

Soviets. Since their breathtaking free programs had equal points, Rodnina and Ulanov could establish a domination that was unchallenged for a decade.

Rodnina's partnership with Ulanov was put under pressure when he fell in love with Lyudmila Smirnova. She was a skater in the Soviet Union's second pairs team. The illusion of romance between Rodnina and Ulanov was shattered when his affair with Smirnova became known during the 1972 Games in Sapporo, Japan. Rodnina knew as she skated off the rink after a gold-medal-winning performance that unless she was very lucky her career was over. There was much concern that a new partner would be very hard to find.

A search was launched throughout the Soviet Union for a new partner for Rodnina. It ended when Aleksandr Zaitsev stepped onto the ice with her. Initially, such was her celebrity status that Zaitsev was too nervous to talk to her. But he matched her extremely well and, though he was by no means an experienced pairs skater, Rodnina liked her new partner. As time went on, however, the pair began to blend personally as well as professionally. The story had a fairy-tale ending when

◀ Irina Rodnina and Aleksei Ulanov skating to victory in the pairs competition in Sapporo, Japan, in 1972. It was their last appearance together because Ulanov soon married another Soviet skater. Rodnina managed to find a brilliant new partner, Aleksandr Zaitsev.

the pair got married.

With her new partner, Rodnina carried on her string of wins. When she took time off to have a baby in 1979 it was after winning her tenth World Championship in a row. In her absence, the World Championship was won by a couple from the United States, Tai Babilonia and Randy Gardner. This suggested that Rodnina's domination was over. But in Lake Placid in 1980, Rodnina came back to win again.

◄ The diminutive Rodnina bounced back and, together with Zaitsev, won another gold medal in Innsbruck in 1976.

▼ The American figure skating team of Tai Babilonia and Randy Gardner.

ICE DANCING

The history of ice dancing is quite separate from pairs skating. It only received Olympic recognition in 1976, although competition in this category goes back a long time.

The history of the sport starts in Austria in about 1870. An American named Jackson Haines went to Europe with skating innovations that proved to be immediately popular. He introduced a boot with a fixed skate, which allowed far greater control and delicacy of movement. Using the popular waltzes of the day, he choreographed attractive set pieces that became widely popular. Haines's fame soon spread all over Europe. He was summoned by Czar Alexander of Russia for private coaching. This, however, was Haines' downfall, for he died in a snowstorm after leaving the palace.

Since ice dancing was elegant and sociable, it was a far more popular sport than pairs skating, which was so physically demanding. Ice dancing was especially popular in Britain in the 1930s. British teams and coaches have dominated the scene ever since.

▼ Jayne Torvill and Christopher Dean flank their coach Betty Callaway as they await the judges' scores at the Sarajevo Games in 1984. The couple won the gold medal.

It was the Soviets, however, who first brought techniques and choreography from ballet to enhance the sport. Their superior presentation made the Soviet teams unbeatable in the 1970s. Skaters around the world watched and learned from them.

Torvill and Dean

Jayne Torvill and Christopher Dean were the couple who, through hard work and imagination, made ice dancing the most famous of all the ice sports.

Both were born in Nottingham, England. The town has a long history of ice skating. They were encouraged to skate from a very young age. Both had other partners until 1974, when they were matched up by Janet Sawbridge, an expert in the sport and a teacher at their local rink. She noted a special compatibility about them. This was also noted by Betty Callaway after they experienced some success. Callaway, an experienced international coach, had an enormous effect on their future.

In 1978 Torvill and Dean won the British National Championships. It was the first time that a local couple had taken the competition, although Nottingham had held the finals since 1950. They quickly became famous locally. But national and international stardom was soon to follow.

Their local celebrity status allowed the two to overcome the disappointment of finishing fifth in the Olympics in Lake Placid in 1980. This had left

▲ Torvill and Dean show off their gold medals. The couple turned professional after the 1984 Games and now perform in lavish shows all over the world.

them with little money or sponsorship opportunities. Thankfully, the local town council offered them a grant. They quickly rewarded this confidence by winning the European Championships in Innsbruck and the World Championships in 1981. Torvill and Dean were then specially honored by the Queen of England, but they had still not reached their peak.

The first unquestionable sign that the couple were in a category of their own was with a routine called *Mack and Mabel*. This was virtually a piece of theater. It was a style of ice dancing that was extremely attractive to the general public, who could not always appreciate the relative difficulty of the moves. They started receiving awards of 6 (the top mark) quite regularly. They were so far ahead of their opponents that only a score of 6 showed the pair was skating to the limit of their ability. The pair competed more against numbers than against other teams. The crowds were pleased by the record-breaking eleven 6s they won for *Mack and Mabel* at the next World Championships.

Their next breathtaking routine was *Barnum on Ice*. However, there was controversy among purists, who felt that ice dancing was becoming too much like pantomime. Torvill and Dean's skill and virtuosity quickly silenced any critics. At the World Championships in Helsinki in 1983, they were awarded nine 6s for artistic impression. Dean revealed afterward that the battle for perfection felt quite separate from the issue of 6s: ''Everyone places so much emphasis on the marks but my thrill was when we went 'boom, boom' at the finish, and the crowds stood for us.''

◄ French-Canadian brother and sister team Isabelle and Paul Duchesnay performing their dramatic routine in Calgary, Canada.

The couple then prepared for the Olympic Games in Sarajevo, Yugoslavia. In the four years since Lake Placid they had reached heights of achievement unknown to any other ice dancers. The Olympics were the stage for the most famous of all their routines, set to the music of Ravel's *Bolero*. A *bolero* is a Spanish dance characterized by its steadily increasing beat and tempo.

Torvill and Dean exploited the slow rhythmical build-up of the piece to suggest growing passion. The romantic elements could not be ignored. Newspapers were full of constant speculations about their personal relationship because they gave off such a strong aura of mutual attraction on the ice. It would not be unkind to say that they fostered this image in the same way Kylie Minogue and Jason Donovan did during their appearances on the Australian television program *Neighbours*. However, there was no evidence of any romantic feelings between them other than those of professional respect and good friendship for each other. Against this, Dean let it be known that he sent Torvill a valentine card.

Torvill and Dean's Olympic routine lasted 4 minutes and 28 seconds. This far exceeded the 4-minute limit. However, nobody complained and they won easily. After this they turned professional. They can still be seen all over the world, performing the routines that made them famous.

▲ Winners of the ice dancing gold medal in Calgary, Soviets Natalia Bestemianova and Andrei Boukine.

SPEEDSKATING

"**S**ome tye bones to their feet . . . and shoving themselves by a little picked staffe, doe slide as swiftly as a bird flyeth."

Speedskating offers a stunning contrast to figure skating and ice dancing. Speedskating is faster and much more robust. Olympic competition takes place outdoors on oval ice tracks that are 400 m long and divided into two lanes. Two skaters compete against the clock and each other, though their times are more important.

Speedskating has a long history, longer indeed than that of any other ice sport. The first recorded speedskating competition took place in England in 1763. There is evidence, however, of the sport taking place as early as the thirteenth century. Dutch paintings of the period show skaters apparently competing against each other. Races were originally held on straight courses. This was because the canals served as fast communication routes. The long tradition of skating in this region goes along with the climate. The flatlands and the dikes often froze to give perfect skating surfaces. In the winter, skating was often the fastest way to get around!

The popularity of the sport spread from England and Holland to Germany,

▼ A group of American speedskaters practicing for the 1924 Games in Chamonix.

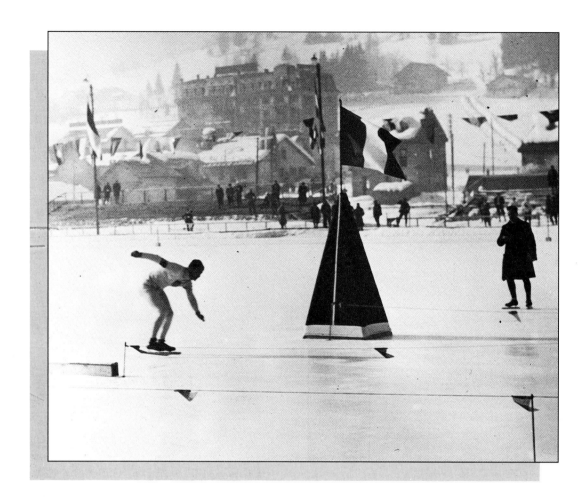

Jewtraw of the United States wins the 500-m speedskating event in 1924.

France, and Austria. In these mountainous regions, skating was virtually a year-round activity because of the frozen conditions at high altitudes.

Early speedskates were no more than animal bones strapped to shoes. Nowadays the speedskates have blades that are 12–18 in (30–46 cm) long and just 6/100 in (1.5 mm) wide.

Speedskaters tend to have very unusual body shapes. They are distinguished by their large thighs, which supply the necessary stamina, and thin upper bodies. One of the most famous speedskaters ever, Eric Heiden, had a

Jewtraw of the United States wins the 500-m speedskating event in 1924.

waist of 32 inches and his thighs measured 29 inches! The original events of 500 m, 1500 m, 5000 m and 10,000 m were supplemented in 1976 by the 1000 m. Since the requirements of the sport in all but the shortest distances are the same, it is not uncommon for one person to win several medals.

The early days of Olympic speedskating competition are marked by the differences that emerged between the

European and American traditions of skating. (It has always been the case that the north Europeans have taken the sport more to their hearts than Americans have. Heiden was actually far more famous in Europe than in America.)

In 1932 the Games were held outside Europe for the first time. In Lake Placid there was a strong challenge to the European skaters by the imposition of North American rules, which included pack skating. This style of physical and tactical racing was unknown to Europeans. Clas Thunberg of Finland, possibly the greatest skater of all time, refused to attend the Games. Born in Helsinki in 1893, Thunberg was virtually a folk hero in his own land. He was thirty-five when he set the world standard of 42.6 seconds for the 500 m and even older when he set records at 1000 m and 3000 m. Except for his personal boycott of the 1932 Games in Lake Placid he might have added more medals to the six medals he had already won.

To add to the problems caused by the pack racing rules, officials insisted that each individual should take the lead at some point in the 10,000-m race. After the initial heats, the fights over this rule and the jostling that had occurred meant they had to be rerun. Then, finally and most ridiculously, in the 1500-m final the judges accused the skaters of "loafing" because the race became tactical for position and hence slow.

Along with Thunberg there are several other Scandinavians who have distinguished their particular country. For Norway the roll of honor includes Bernt Evensen, 500-m champion in 1928, and Hjalmar Andersen, who in 1952 won the 1500 m, 5000 m, and 10,000 m. His victory in the 5000 m was by a margin of 11 seconds!

▼ Hjalmar "Hjallis" Andersen of Norway speeds along in the 5000-m event held at the Bislett Stadium in Oslo in 1952. In winning the event, Andersen clipped 9 seconds off the Olympic record. His time was 8 minutes 10.6 seconds, which was 3.3 seconds below his own world record.

Of all the champions who have won more than one gold medal, perhaps the greatest was Eric Heiden. Heiden came to prominence as the sensational winner of the 1977 World Championships. He went on to win in 1978 and 1979. He set his first world record in the 3000 m in 1978. By the time of the Olympic finals there was no one to touch him. In all events except for the shortest, the 500 m, he was so

▲ Yevgeny Kulikov of the Soviet Union won the men's 500-m speedskating title in Innsbruck in 1976.

► The powerful and muscular physique of the remarkable Eric Heiden. Heiden is considered the greatest speedskater of all time.

dominant that the *New York Times* wrote memorably that Heiden was "... to ice what (Mark) Spitz is to

chlorinated water." Nothing though is ever so easy. And Heiden certainly had a fair share of luck in winning more individual golds than the great Spitz.

In his worst event, the 500 m, he was paired against the world record holder Yevgeny Kulikov of the Soviet Union. Luckily for Heiden, Kulikov slipped. Heiden turned in the better time in what turned out to be the fastest pairing. The night before the 10,000-m final he attended the famous ice hockey match between the United States and the Soviet Union. Excited by the spectacle, he slept badly. However, he went into the competition more determined than ever to win. Heiden broke the existing record by 6 seconds.

The speedskating star of the 1980s was Tomas Gustafson. The brilliant Swede first came to prominence at the 1984 Games in Sarajevo when he won the 5000 m. Four years later in Calgary, Gustafson took 51.7 seconds off the 10,000-m world record.

The first women's competition took place in 1960. The first great star was Lydia Skoblikova who won six golds in the 500 m, 1000 m, 1500 m, and 3000 m. Sheila Young of the United States won the 500-m title in 1976. She also won the bronze in the 1000 m and the silver in the 1500 m. This made Young the first American to win a complete set of Winter Olympic medals in a single Games. As if this wasn't enough, later in the year she won the World Amateur Sprint Cycle Championship!

▲ Heiden powers along the ice track in the 10,000-m final at the 1980 Games in Lake Placid. He went on to win the gold medal. It was yet another medal in this brilliant Olympian's career. Heiden's case is a typical example of how competitors and events in the Winter Games are regarded as secondary to their counterparts, the Summer Games. Heiden won more individual gold medals than Mark Spitz. But who is most remembered?

▶ American Sheila Young rounds the bend to victory in the women's 500-m speedskating final in 1976 in Innsbruck.

GLOSSARY

Artificial Something that is not natural and has been man-made.

Censure To find fault with something or condemn it as being wrong.

Choreography The way in which dances are arranged.

Compulsory Something that one must do.

Diminutive Very small.

Featherweight Someone who weighs less than 126 lb (57 kg).

Friction The rubbing of the surface of one object against another.

Invincible Something or someone who cannot be defeated.

Phenomenon Any person, thing, or event that is very unusual or remarkable.

Puck A hard rubber disk used in ice hockey.

Seeded In a competition, the top athletes are seeded in order of ability to win. For example, the athlete who is considered the best will be seeded number one.

Shutout When a goalkeeper does not let in any goals in an ice hockey game.

Tenacity Showing stubbornness and persistence.

Triple Crown Winning the World, Olympic, and European titles in the same season.

Veteran Someone who has a lot of experience.

Vulnerable Liable to be hurt or harmed in some way.

FURTHER READING

Frommer, Harvey. *Olympic Controversies.* New York: Franklin Watts, 1987.

Glubock, Shirley, and Alfred Tamarin. *Olympic Games in Ancient Greece.* New York: Harper Junior Books, 1976.

Greenberg, Stan, ed. *The Guinness Book of Olympic Facts and Feats.* New York: Bantam, 1984.

Marshall, Nancy Thies. *Women Who Compete.* Old Tappan, N.J.: Fleming H. Revell Company, 1988.

Tatlow, Peter. *The Olympics.* New York: Franklin Watts, 1988.

Walczewski, Michael. *The Olympic Fun Fact Book.* New York: Dell, 1988.

Wallechinsky, David. *The Complete Book of the Olympics.* New York: Penguin Books, 1988.

INDEX

Numbers in **bold** refer to captions.